REBELS

102900.252118.000012   GHOST SHIP   001035.10

STAR WARS   STAR WARS

Radar Function

001000   11   10

4

THE
INQUISITOR'S TRAP

Based on the episode "Rise of the Old Masters,"
written by Henry Gilroy

Adapted by Meredith Rusu

© & TM 2014 Lucasfilm Ltd.

Published by Disney • Lucasfilm Press, an imprint of Disney Book Group. No part of
this book may be reproduced or transmitted in any form or by any means, electronic
or mechanical, including photocopying, recording, or by any information storage
and retrieval system, without written permission from the publisher. For information
address Disney • Lucasfilm Press, 1101 Flower Street, Glendale, California 91201.

Printed in China
First Edition, December 2014
1 3 5 7 9 10 8 6 4 2

ISBN 978-1-4847-2609-9
T425-2382-5-14356

Visit the official *Star Wars* website at: www.starwars.com
This book was printed on paper created from a sustainable source.

LUCASFILM
P R E S S

Los Angeles • New York

"Focus on letting go," Kanan instructed Ezra.

"Letting go? Rather hold on, if you don't mind." Ezra tried to stay balanced in a handstand on top of the *Ghost* . . . which was hovering above a high mountain!

Kanan was teaching Ezra to use the Force. But so far, the lesson wasn't going well. Next to them, Chopper beeped with excitement. It was time for Ezra to practice using Kanan's lightsaber, and the little droid was eager to "help."

Chopper sent a flurry of empty jugs shooting toward Ezra. No matter how hard Ezra tried, he couldn't deflect all of them. As jug after jug hit him, he toppled over the edge of the ship!

Kanan used the Force to pull Ezra back up just in time. As they entered the *Ghost*, he confronted Ezra: "You weren't focused."

"Tough to focus when I'm falling to my death," Ezra said sarcastically.

Kanan sighed. "It's difficult to teach," the Jedi said quietly. Then he walked away.

Ezra felt hurt. He was trying his best to learn to be a Jedi. Was Kanan *that* disappointed in him?

Suddenly, Hera called out from the common room: "Kanan, come see this!"

Everyone gathered around to hear a new message on the ship's holonet broadcaster.

"Citizens, this is Senator-in-Exile Gall Trayvis. I bring you news the Empire doesn't want you to hear. Jedi Master Luminara Unduli is alive!"

Kanan gasped. "If Master Luminara is alive, we must rescue her. She was a great Jedi Master." Kanan looked at Ezra. "She'd make an excellent teacher for you."

Ezra's heart sank even further. Kanan didn't want to train him anymore!

"He's done with me," Ezra mumbled bitterly.

Soon the *Ghost* was speeding toward a stormy planet. The senator's broadcast had said that Master Luminara was being held there in a deadly prison called the Spire.

Kanan pointed to a spot on the prison schematics. "This is where we'll sneak in. We'll make our way to the upper-level isolation cells, free Luminara, and come back out the way we came in."

"You'd have to be crazy to try that crazy plan," Sabine said with a half smile.

Kanan nodded. "Let's hope the Empire thinks so, too."

Thick clouds surrounded the Spire when the rebels arrived. Silently, Hera piloted their stealth ship, the *Phantom*, just above the prison, staying hidden in the mist.

Ezra, Kanan, Zeb, and Sabine parachuted from the ship to a guard platform and crept inside the Spire.

Sabine hacked into the prison's computers. "Luminara's being held in cell 0169 on the lower level," she said.

Kanan frowned. "That's not where we thought she'd be. We planned off of outdated schematics."

"What does that mean?" Ezra asked.

"It means the plan changes," Kanan said grimly.

Kanan and Ezra went to find Master Luminara's cell while Zeb and Sabine stood guard at their escape point.

"Once we free Master Luminara, she will be able to teach you," Kanan said quietly to Ezra, "much better than I could."

Ezra scowled. *Guess Kanan can't wait to ditch me,* he thought.

Soon they reached cell 0169. Inside, Master Luminara floated unconscious in a stasis field.

"Is it really her?" Ezra asked.

"Yes . . ." Kanan said slowly. "But something's wrong."

Suddenly, the stasis field—and Master Luminara—disappeared. It was just a hologram. Ezra and Kanan had walked into a trap!

"I don't understand . . ." Kanan gasped in disbelief.

"No? It doesn't seem complicated," a voice echoed behind them.

The cell door slammed. Kanan and Ezra wheeled around to face a shadowy man dressed in long black robes. A red lightsaber hummed in his hand.

"I am the Inquisitor," the man said with a smile. "Welcome."

Kanan attacked the Inquisitor with his lightsaber, trying to protect Ezra. But he was no match for the dark warrior's power.

"Is that all you've got?" the Inquisitor sneered.

Ezra pointed to the cell door. "We've got *this*." He had attached an explosive device to the door. Ezra pressed the detonator. *BOOM!*

Ezra and Kanan dashed out of the cell. The Inquisitor was right on their heels. He used the Force to push Kanan away from Ezra.

"Your 'master' cannot save you, boy," the Inquisitor said. "He is unfocused and undisciplined."

"Then we're perfect for each other," Ezra shot back.

The Inquisitor chuckled. "I do so admire your persistence. Ready to die?"

"*No!*" Kanan used the last ounce of his strength to Force-smash the Inquisitor into the ceiling. Then, together, Ezra and Kanan escaped.

"Guys, this way!" Sabine cried as Kanan and Ezra raced up to her and Zeb. The friends hurried toward the giant door leading to the landing platform where they had come in. But the entire prison was in lockdown. The door was sealed shut!

Calmly, Kanan turned to Ezra. "It's up to us to use the Force to unlock the door," he said.

"Seriously?" Ezra asked. Now didn't seem like the time for a lesson.

But Ezra closed his eyes and focused on the lock with Kanan. Suddenly, the door sprang open. Ezra couldn't believe it. They had done it!

Together, the friends battled the stormtroopers on the platform to reach the *Phantom*, and they leaped aboard.

The Inquisitor seethed as he watched them escape. This would not be the last time they would meet.

On board, Hera looked at Kanan. "Master Luminara?" she
asked.

Kanan shook his head. "Gone. We'll have to find a way to
spread the word."

Hera nodded. She knew how much it had meant to Kanan
to find the old Jedi Master.

A few days later, docked safely on a grassy planet, the friends watched a new holonet broadcast.

"Citizens, I regret to inform you that Master Luminara is gone. But I urge you to keep her memory alive."

When the broadcast ended, Kanan turned to look at Ezra, but the boy wasn't there.

Kanan went outside and found Ezra sitting on the entry ramp.

"Don't bother saying it," Ezra said before Kanan could speak. "I know you wanted to dump me on Luminara. Just because she's gone doesn't mean you're stuck with me."

Kanan was shocked.

"Ezra," Kanan said with a sigh. "I don't want to dump you. I just wanted you to have the best teacher. But now I see that if I don't believe I can teach you, then I won't succeed. So from now on, I *will* teach you. There is no try."

Ezra's face broke into a wide grin as Kanan tossed him his lightsaber.

Kanan smiled back. "Shall we begin?"

REBELS
GHOST SHIP
STAR
WARS
Rebel